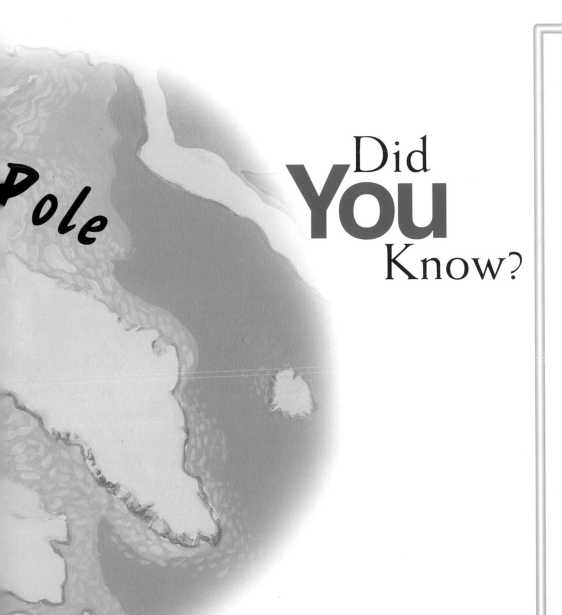

Pole

Did YOU Know?

- During the Arctic winter, the temperature can drop to −50F.

- Far north of the Arctic Circle, the sun doesn't rise for 50 or more winter days!

- The Arctic tundra has a layer of permanently frozen soil, called permafrost.

- The Arctic tundra gets as little precipitation (rain and snow) as many deserts!

- Many Arctic animals develop white coats that help them hide in winter.

- Snow actually helps some animals keep warm!

For Noah, who warms me through the coldest winters
Virginia Kroll

For my kids, Wolf and Teal
Michael S. Maydak

Message to Parents

Bear & Company, part of The Boyds Collection, Ltd. family, is committed to creating quality reading and play experiences that inspire kids to learn, imagine, and explore the world around them. Working together with experienced children's authors, illustrators, and educators, we promise to create stories and products that are respectful to your children and that will earn your respect in turn.

Published by Bear & Company Publications
Copyright © 2002 by Bear & Company

All rights reserved. No part of this book may be reproduced or used in any manner whatsoever without written permission. For information regarding permission, write to:
Permissions
Bear & Company Publications
P.O. Box 3876
Gettysburg, PA 17325

Printed in the United States of America
My Home™ is a registered trademark of Bear & Company.

Based on a series concept by Dawn Jones
Edited by Dawn Jones
Designed by Vernon Thornblad

Library of Congress Cataloging-in-Publication Data
Kroll, Virginia L.
  Flurry's frozen tundra / written by Virginia Kroll ; illustrated by Michael S. Maydak.
      p. cm. -- (My home ; 2)
"Based on a series concept by Dawn L. Jones."
Summary: At the end of a hard winter an arctic fox steals food from a polar bear, finds himself in trouble, and must be rescued by his friends, who suggest that he patiently await summer and its abundance of food. Includes facts about animals of the tundra.
  ISBN 0-9712840-4-0 (alk. paper)
[1. Arctic fox--Fiction. 2. Foxes--Fiction. 3. Tundra animals--Fiction. 4. Hunger--Fiction. 5. Tundras--Fiction.] I. Maydak, Michael S., ill. II. Jones, Dawn L., 1963- III. Title.
  PZ7.K9227 Fl 2001
  [E]--dc21
                                             2001005150

Flurry's Frozen Tundra

By Virginia Kroll   Illustrated by Michael S. Maydak

bear&
company

1

In the North, almost at the top of the world, there's a place where winter seems to last forever. Cyclones of snow swirl with sudden windy gusts. Ice glistens as far as the eye can see. From a distance, this flat, smooth world of white seems empty. But a closer look reveals the snowy tracks of the animals that live there. Their bodies are working hard to keep them warm....

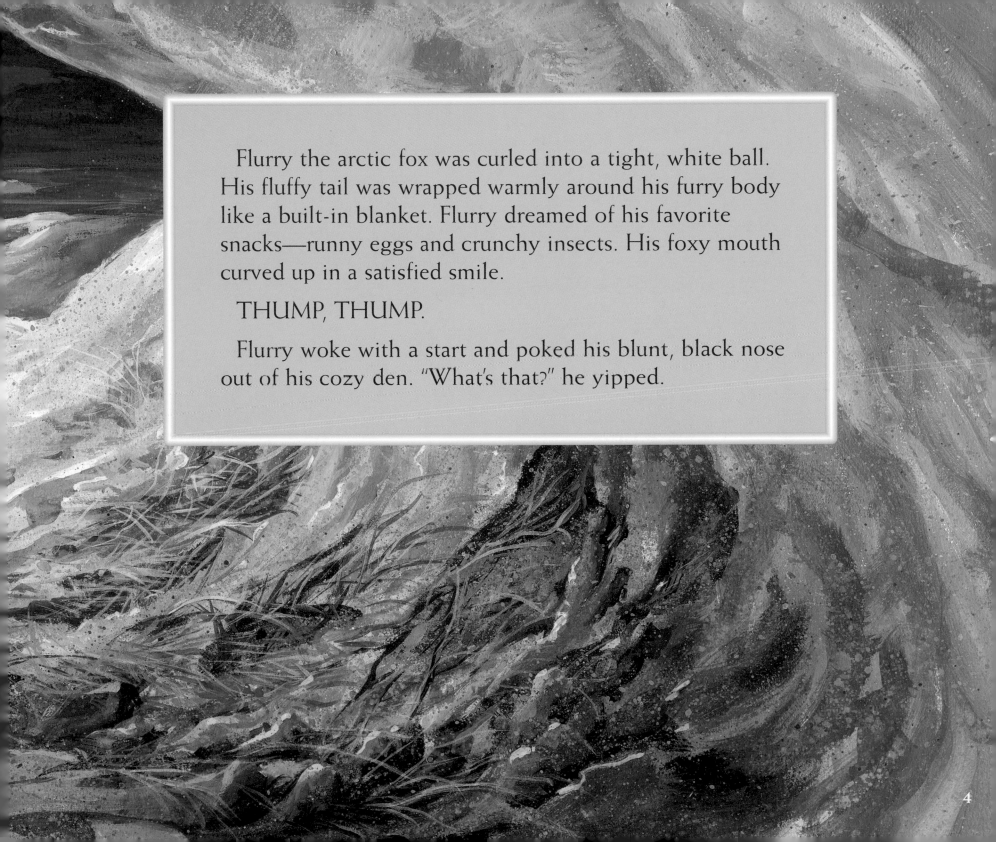

Flurry the arctic fox was curled into a tight, white ball. His fluffy tail was wrapped warmly around his furry body like a built-in blanket. Flurry dreamed of his favorite snacks—runny eggs and crunchy insects. His foxy mouth curved up in a satisfied smile.

THUMP, THUMP.

Flurry woke with a start and poked his blunt, black nose out of his cozy den. "What's that?" he yipped.

Oomingmak the musk ox lifted her heavy hoof and thumped again. "There is a clump of dried grass under this snow. I just know it," she said, scraping the ground. "Ah, there." She pulled the grass up with her mighty lips and mumbled to Flurry through her munching. "Would you care for a blade?"

Flurry's tummy rumbled. "I am hungry, but not for grasses," he grumbled. "I need a meaty meal. An egg or two or an insect or three would suit me."

"Just thought I'd offer," said Oomingmak. "It's the end of winter. You know how hard it is to find food."

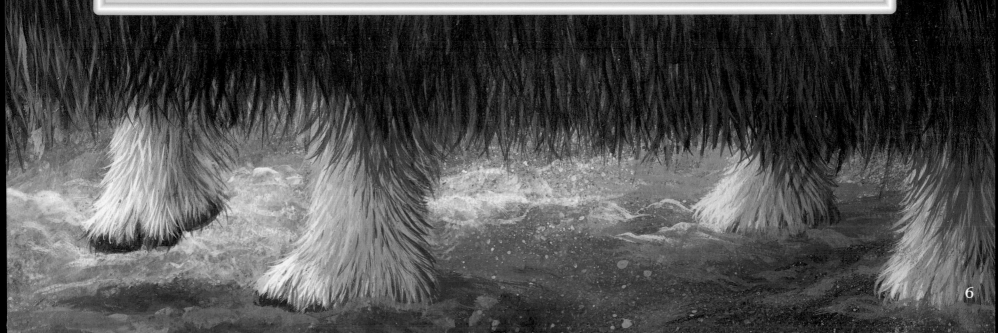

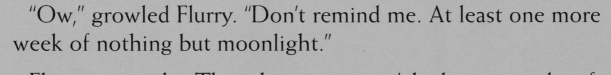

"Ow," growled Flurry. "Don't remind me. At least one more week of nothing but moonlight."

Flurry was right. Though it was two o'clock on a tundra afternoon, the only light on the frozen landscape came from the pale glow of the moon and the white of the snow. All the creatures, including Flurry, called their home the "Beautiful Land." But this winter had been harder than most.

Flurry had even heard complaints from the polar bear, whom they all called Mighty One. He usually liked winter best of all. But even Mighty One had found it hard to get around with all the extra-blinding blizzards.

8

"Freeze!" ordered Oomingmak.

"What do you mean, 'freeze'?" said Flurry. "It's fifty degrees below zero. I'm already freezing."

"I mean, don't move," answered Oomingmak. "Mighty One is passing by. If he hears, sees, or smells us, I'll have to call my herd for help."

Flurry thought that Oomingmak and her herd had the best way of helping each other. When danger was near, they formed a circle with tails in and faces out. Calves and weaker oxen stayed in the center. Those on the outside would stomp and snort and shake their huge, hard-horned heads.

I'll bet even Mighty One would be afraid of them, Flurry thought.

Flurry was still hungry, but thinking about Mighty One gave him an idea. "I'll follow him to his hunting hole," he said, smiling at his own cleverness. "Then, when he isn't looking, I'll snatch a scrap and have a mini feast!"

12

Oomingmak frowned at her fearless friend. "You know how angry Mighty One gets when someone else tries to steal food that he's worked hard to catch," she warned. "You may be fast, but you're no match for him. Why don't you wait for summer? You still have a little of last year's fat under your skin to give you energy."

"I agree. I agree," called Snowy the snowy owl from a nearby hill. "Even with my swift wings, I'd never sneak up on Mighty One. He's always alert. One swipe of his claws would wipe you out. Why, one chomp of his terrible teeth could make a snack of you!"

Flurry's tummy growled again. "You'll see. Mighty One won't catch me," he said. Then he dashed off toward the frozen ocean.

Snowy clacked his beak, and Oomingmak bowed her great, brown head.

When Flurry reached the ice, Mighty One was busy. He had a fresh-caught meal, the first food he'd found in a long time.

Quick as lightning, Flurry snatched a piece from the ground. He raced away before Mighty One realized he'd been underfoot. Flurry ducked behind a big ice bank and gobbled, ignoring Mighty One's chilling roar.

"Oh-ho," said Wrinkle the walrus, who was resting on a nearby ice chunk. "You may have escaped once, but you won't escape twice. Now Mighty One will be on the lookout for you. It's safer to catch your own food."

Flurry smacked his lips over every tasty bit. "That's easy for you to say. You can eat clams from the ocean floor. You have tusks for digging them up and blubber to keep you warm underwater. But what can I do? It's easier to snatch a bit from Mighty One than to waste my energy hunting. After all, I'm weak from not eating."

"Suit yourself," said Wrinkle. She waddled away on all four flippers to join her whiskered family.

The next day, Flurry felt braver than ever. He watched Mighty One catch another meal. Then he crept behind the huge bear and grabbed a piece of meat!

"Watch out!" blurted Wrinkle from her ice chunk.

Flurry turned on his quick feet, but it was too late. Mighty One had spotted him. The small fox was no match for the huge, white paw.

Flurry tripped on the ice. "Ow!" he howled. A heavy claw grabbed a tuft of fur from his fluffy tail. "Help!"

Suddenly, Flurry saw a bright-white flash. "Follow me," screeched Snowy. The owl flew low, zigzagging out of Mighty One's reach, with Flurry right behind him.

Flurry ran faster than he ever knew he could. When he looked back, he saw Mighty One almost on top of him.

"Look! Up ahead!" screamed Snowy as Flurry sped along.

"Oh, no!" Flurry yapped. There was a solid wall of brown in front of him. But he couldn't stop.

"Through my legs," shouted Oomingmak.

It wasn't a wall after all! It was a circle of safety!

Flurry sped through Oomingmak's legs to the center of the circle. From there, he peeked out, nudging aside his friend's ice-fringed skirt. Oomingmak and her family surrounded him. They faced out, snorting, stomping, and showing their thick, curved horns to Mighty One.

The bear reared up on two legs and bellowed. Then he bounded away, back to the ice to finish his food.

After the danger was past, Snowy sat on Oomingmak's back. Flurry thanked them both. "That was a close call," he said.

He looked at his slightly less fluffy tail and shuddered. "Lose a tuft, learn a lesson," he added. "I won't be foolish enough to steal from Mighty One again. I guess I'll just wait for summer, like everyone else."

Snowy hooted. "You won't have to wait long. Listen."

28

Flurry opened his small, round ears and heard the honking.

"Look," said Oomingmak in a hopeful voice. A flock of snow geese made a ribbon across the sky. "They always bring the summer with them."

As she spoke, the moon faded and the horizon grew bright with the promise of sunshine.

Flurry yipped for joy and wagged what was left of his fluffy tail. "Beautiful Land indeed," he said, thinking about the warm, well-fed days of summer ahead.

His friends agreed.

The **Arctic tundra** is a cold, dry, and treeless territory just below the ice cap of the North Pole. Long winters of snow and harsh temperatures as low as 25 degrees below zero (F) can last from September to May.

More About the Arctic Tundra

Arctic foxes, snowy owls, and the other types of animals featured in this story really do live on the frozen tundra. They don't talk to one another the way that Flurry, Oomingmak, Snowy, and Wrinkle do in *Flurry's Frozen Tundra*, but they face the same dangers and behave in similar ways. Read more about these fascinating animals....

During a **brief summer,** when the sun almost never sets, the top layer of tundra soil unfreezes. The ground explodes with grasses, colorful flowers, and low shrubs. This is a well-fed time for the animals that live there, very different from the bleak winter, when the sun rarely rises and food is harder to find.

Musk oxen, like Oomingmak, are large, cow-like animals. They have thick, shaggy overcoats for warmth and woolly, waterproof layers underneath. They live on the tundra year-round and use their large, curved hooves to paw through winter snow to search for buried grasses and twigs. They really do make "circles of safety."

Oomingmak *is the native peoples' name for the musk ox. It means "Bearded One."*

Arctic foxes like Flurry, have small faces and short, round ears that help save body heat. They are well-prepared for the cold weather with large, furry, snowshoe feet and white winter coats with two layers for extra warmth. When asleep, they can wrap their large tails around themselves for even more warmth.

Snowy owls, like Snowy, live year-round on the tundra. Their feathers help keep them warm and sometimes even cover their bills and clawed feet. The males are almost completely white, which helps them hide in the snow and ice. When scared, a snowy owl makes a call that sounds like sharp barks.

Walruses, like Wrinkle, are well-built for life in the cold sea, with a thick layer of fatty blubber to help keep them warm. They use their strong tusks to dig favorite foods from the ocean floor—clams, mussels, and sea snails.

Of all the bears, **polar bears,** such as Mighty One, are the most outstanding hunters. Well-hidden against ice and snow by a pure white coat, a polar bear usually hunt seals, its favorite food. It will also eat fish, seaweed, grass, birds, and other arctic animals. Polar bears do not go south in winter, but may travel for several miles in search of food.

Where in the World Is the Arctic Tundra?

The North

The **Arctic tundra** is a cold, dry, and treeless territory just below the ice cap of the **North Pole**. Tundra covers **10%** of the earth.